Smart Alec Alex

The Vacation from...
Hello — Operator, Help!

Copyright © 2020 by Taunya D. Said

First edition 2020

Illustrations by FX AND COLOR STUDIO
www.fxandcolorstudio.com
Book design by Tobi Carter
Edited by Debbie Manber Kupfer

ISBN 979-8-5560-7400-2 (paperback)

Smart Alec Alex

The Vacation from...
Hello — Operator, Help!

By T. D. Said

This book is dedicated to my Grandmother,
Laura Virginia Woolfolk
R.I.H.

This book is a remembrance of you and the scary
antics you use to do (LOL).

As I reflect on my life, I am thankful for our long
talks. You believed in me and you showered me with
your encouraging words and blessings in everything
I do. I know you are my guardian angel, for I feel
your presence. I hope I've made you proud.

I love you and miss you very much.

Contents

Get your read on,
dudes and dudettes!

We'll see you at the end.

Chapter One

Off to Grandma's House We Go, Go, Ghost!

Hey diddle dee, everybody, it's me, Alexandria P. Knowitall. Oh brother, not again. My thick-head brother, Andrew, is watching basketball, and his television is too loud. Every time I want to tell you dudes and dudettes a story, I can't hear myself think. I better close my door.

{{Slam!}}

Okay, now sit back and relax while I tell you what happened to me and my BFFs a week ago on Spring Break.

For weeks, Candice and I talked about what we wanted to do on spring break. I wanted to go camping. Candice wanted to go to a hair show. Oh brother!

Calvin wanted to collect bugs, and Sissy just wanted to hang around the city sports and learning center.

"What to do, what to do, we can't decide on anything," I said.

"Well, little Ms. I'll-be-bored, if you can't decide, how about we go on a vacation to the swamp country," suggested Mom.

"Ugh, that sounds boring," I pouted.

"How about you bring your little crew, Candice, Sissy, and Calvin?" said Mom.

Whew! Mom allowed me to take my BFFs. What a life saver!

My Budster's (friends) asked their parents if they could go, and their parents were okie dokie with it, yay!

All night, I thought about where we were going and how unfair it was that my big-head, brother, Andrew, didn't have to go. He got to stay the week with his friends at a basketball camp that had everything. The camp was taking the kids to an amusement park and best of all, swimming!

I guess you're wondering why I wasn't going to a spring camp. Well, I've been to camp every year, and I wanted to do something different.

But for the life of me, I just couldn't seem to get excited about this year's activity.

The day arrived and the gang were all here on time and ready for our adventure. We shoved

our duffle bags in the trunk of the car, and Mom placed her nice designer bag with all her stuff in it in the trunk. Ooo, fancy!

"Mrs. K, I love your bag!" Candice notices that kind of stuff.

We were on our way to Wood Crack, Louisiana near the creepy bayou. Over the hills, and through the woods, across the sluggish body of water to … youuuu guessed it, Grandma's house!

My mom was born there, SMH! That place is hot and creepy. You see I'd been there before, but I was too young to remember if I was scared or not. But I have pictures of the house for proof, LOL.

Anyway, it's been a long time since we'd seen Grandma Gheema. In a picture my mom showed me, Grandma is as pale as a ghost. Or at least that's what she looks like to me, very creepy. Wait until my BFFs see her.

"Mom, how long is this ride going to be? It feels like we've been riding for ten hours, and I'm tired."

"Alex honey, be patient and enjoy the ride. We will be there in two naps of a turtle's tail."

"How do you know that, Mrs. Knowitall, How do you know?" Calvin asked.

"Calvin, don't bother Mrs. K. I can't wait until we get there. We are going to have so much fun." Sissy laughed.

"I hope I don't sweat my hair out. If we are going to a swampy place, I'm sure I will start to look a mess in no time," Candice complained.

"Yes, I know, I know, but what else is new, princess?" That Candice, she's always goes on about her hair and stuff

"Kids behave yourself. We are almost there," Mom said.

It was beginning to get dark as we rode along the lonely dusty road. I looked for signs, but there weren't any in sight, so how did Mom know where she was going? We were heading down into the bayou, and the trees towering over the dirt road blocked the daylight making it look like it was nighttime.

Suddenly Calvin started to stutter, which was nothing new for him, and pointed toward the front of the car. We noticed something white on the road in front of us, but it was too far ahead for us to see what it was. As we slowly approached it, we realized it was a strange looking white dog with only three legs. His eyes were red, and his teeth looked very sharp. I was a little shaken and so were my BFFs. Sissy wasn't laughing like she usually did, Candice was quiet, and Calvin was scared silly with his eyes wide open. I couldn't imagine what was going through their heads at that moment. Yet Mom was still driving as if nothing was wrong. As we passed the strange looking white dog, I looked back and noticed that it wasn't there anymore. It was like he had disappeared into thin air; I didn't understand!

"Aaalex, maybe we should have stayed home," Candice whispered.

"Oh, Popsicle sticks! Stop your whining, dudette," I said.

I didn't want to admit it, but I thought Candice was right.

We arrived at Grandma Gheema's house in time for dinner.

Chapter Two

Welcome, My Little Lovelies

Good grief, these guys were not going to be happy when they saw what we had to do to get over to Grandma's house.

"Alex, why is there a small, old, rusty boat at the dock over there and no road to your granny's house?" Candice asked.

"Umm, well, you see, we have to take that small, old, rusty boat across the bayou to get to Grandma's house. That's the only way there," I explained

"Huh, what, wait! You're kidding, right?" Candice looked horrified.

"NOPE, not kidding!"

"Okay, kids, grab your things, and let's skedaddle across the swamp. Calvin, you can help me row the boat," Mom said.

"Yes Mrs. K, yes ma'am. I can help; I can help you row, row the boat."

Calvin was as scared as a frog hopping across a busy highway running from a snake.

"Oh my goodness, it is too hot out here. My cherry, lemon, raspberry, bubblegum lip-gloss is going to melt. I can't breathe," Candice whined.

"Hey, dudettes, don't leave me!"

Sissy hurried into the boat with her pant legs rolled up to her knees.

"Alex dear, come on, what are you doing?"

"Mom, do we *have* to take this grim-reaping boat to get across to Grandma's house?"

"Yesss, Ms. Missy. Now, come on."

"But I don't want to go across this icky water. What if the gator monster jumps out and grabs us?" I said.

"GATOR MONSTER!" the gang yelled.

"Wait, there's a gator monster?" said Candice.

"Yes, dudettes, but I'm too important to be captured," I joked.

I could see Grandma Gheema waiting for us to reach her house on the other side of the swamp. She was standing on a half-broken pier waving.

"I hope she doesn't fall." I said.

"Grandma Gheema looks like she could put a spell on you." Sissy laughed.

"What, what do you, you mean, Sissy?" Calvin looked scared.

Sissy threw her hands out and wiggled her fingers at Calvin.

"Hey! Cut it out, you guys," I said.

"I know the fearless Smart Alec Alex isn't scared, is she?" Sissy taunted.

"Whatever, Sillington," I said.

"Can we just get this over with?" Candice said.

"Hey! hey kids, come on, let's get a move on. Calvin, can you row a little faster?" said Mom.

The house looked incredibly old with chunks of chipped paint falling off. In fact, the house looked haunted. There were tiny green tree vines all over the walls, so that it appeared like the house was being swallowed by the forest. I turned around to look at Mom, who was waving at Grandma Gheema, but even she looked weird. It was as if my mom was turning as white as my grandma. It occurred to me that she was back in her original element.

"Mm, Mom, are you okay?" I murmured.

"Why, Alex dear, of course," answered Mom in a soft and shaky voice with a slight glow in her eyes.

I reared back with a what's-wrong-with-her look on my face. My BFFs could see that the coolest kid in T.K. Spittle Middle School was a bit spooked. But if you know me the way you should by now, I always play it cool as a cucumber, ha ha.

"It sure is scary out here, Alex. I'm not too sure about this little visit with your grandmother in the middle of a swampy creek. This is not what we had in mind for fun!" Candice looked terrified.

"Oh buddy, oh pal, oh chum! We're going to have a blast, there's nothing to worry about." I tried to reassure her.

Still in the back of my mind, I was a little worried. I hoped this trip would be fine and that it would be over in no time.

Sissy, being the silly one in the bunch, cracked jokes all the way across the swamp while trying to hide her nervousness, but everyone knows that when Sissy is nervous, she starts talking too much and too fast. I call her motormouth sometimes.

As we approached the pier, Grandma's eyes took on a yellow glow, and she greeted us with a witchy grin.

"Whoa, did you see that?" said Sissy.

"What, what," asked Calvin.

"Her eyes, they are glowing," Sissy explained.

Calvin was shaking and biting his fingernails.

"Welcome, my lovelies! Welcome to Grandma Gheema's home," said Grandma, cackling.

We all jumped out of the creepy boat.

"Yucky mucky, this is a mess!" I screamed out loud.

"Alex, dear, don't make such a fuss, come in and have some of Grandma Gheema's cookies."

"Cookies, yay! Cookies, I love cookies," Sissy said.

"He he he, what a little firecracker, you are," Grandma Gheema giggled.

"Oh dear, what, what, what is that on the porch, on the porch?" said a nervous Calvin.

"I don't know, Calvin. It looks like a dog," Sissy said.

"Whoa, it looks like the same white dog we saw on that dark road," Candice said.

Me and my BFFs tiptoed by the strange looking dog. Suddenly, the dog opened its eyes and started to howl like a wolf glaring at the moon.

"I don't know, I don't know about you guys, but, but I'm scared. I want to go home," Calvin said.

Grandma Gheema gently bent down and looked Calvin in the eyes and said, "Aww, I want you to stay with me, my little gumdrop".

Me, Sissy, Calvin, and Candice entered the old scary house in the creepy forest in the bayou. We were all amazed by the many artifacts (things Grandma made) on the floor. It was almost like a museum of dolls.

The handcrafted dolls looked like they were alive and little did we know…. they were! When I walked by a doll its head would turn. Did I see what I thought I saw? I was afraid to say anything. If I did, my friends would think I was a nutty buddy.

Chapter Three

Dinner with Uncle Roscoe

"So, what have you conjured up for dinner, Mother?" asked Mom.

"Ahhh! I have a special treat for you all. Let Grandma Gheema check on dinner, and we can eat in two shakes of a rattlesnake's tail. I've got Uncle Roscoe coming by. He's gonna bless the food," said Grandma Gheema.

"I hope she's made hamburgers and hot dogs," Sissy blurted out. "I love hamburgers and hot dogs!"

And in the midst of her excitement Sissy did a cartwheel and landed near the ghostly white dog that she'd thought was still outside. The dog licked his lips. She swiftly jumped up and moved out of his way.

No one was saying anything, and it was very quiet, then out of nowhere we heard a chant, "Flimb Flam Kaboo, I'm going to feed the kids this stew, and for those reading this book....... there's plenty to go around for you too!"

Grandma laughed and laughed as she stirred the pot of what she called poor man's stew.

There was a knock on the door, and we all turned around.

"Ha Haaa! Hiya, family." Uncle Roscoe waved from the back screen-door. "Glad to see you made it down these parts.

Gheema said ya'll were coming.

Well, you must be Patricia. I haven't seen you since you were knee high to a tadpole. And who do we have here? Are all these your crumb snatchers, Patricia?"

"Hey there, Uncle Roscoe. No, this is my daughter, Alex, and her friends, Candice, Calvin, and Sissy. You may as well call them my kids; they are always together."

"Well alrighty then, so which one of these tadpoles is Alex?"

"That would be me, Alexandria P. Knowitall." I took a bow.

"Well happy to meet you, Pumpkin!" Uncle Roscoe said.

"Hey kids, I'm everybody's Uncle Roscoe."

My BFFs waved.

"Gather your belonging and I'll show you to your rooms," Mom said.

Everyone started upstairs. The house was huge and full of spider webs.

"Does anyone clean this place?" Candice said.

"Okay, Alex, you, Sissy and Candice are in the PeaPod room, and Calvin you'll be across the hall from the girls in the Low Toad room," Mom said.

"Mom, why do the rooms have names?"

"I'm not sure. It's been like this since I was a kid."

"Um, Mmmrs. Kkk, doooo, do I have to stay in a room all alone?" Calvin mumbled.

"Well, Calvin, you can't possibly think I'm going to put you in a room with a bunch of girls, do you?"

Calvin looked very disappointed.

"Pull up your big boy pants. You'll be fine," Mom said.

"Oh, Calvin! You will be fine. I can't have you looking at my girlie stuff," Candice said.

"We girls have to stick together. Boys—yuck!" Sissy said.

"Being the only boy, only boy, sucks! I wish there was another dude, another dude, in this clan," Calvin said.

"Hey diddle diddle, I have the bed in the middle," Sissy said.

"Hey, wait a minute, this is my grandma's house, so I get to choose first," I said loud and proud.

"Alex, I'm scared. I want to be in the middle of you and Sissy," said Candice.

"Oh please, let the fancy pants sleep in the middle, I don't care. We're all here together," Sissy said.

"Okay, dudette, we have your back," I said.

"When you guys settle down and have put your clothes away, come down for dinner," Mom said.

After about twenty minutes, Mom called for us to come and eat.

I sniffed the air. "Something doesn't smell right!"

All four of us stepped into the hallway and sniffed. We walked pass the scary pictures and downstairs to the large dining room, only to discover there are animal heads all around the walls of the room.

"I guess someone in this house is a headhunter," Sissy said, laughing.

We all sat down.

Grandma Gheema placed bowls of soup in front of Calvin, Sissy, Candice, and me.

Grandma Gheema turned to my uncle. "Roscoe, go on and bless the food."

"Alright now, Ha ha! Bless this food, oh Father, and bless the hands that prepared it too. Let this time our food stand still, please Father, no movement. I can't take no mo surprises, so bless this delicious soup, Wonder, Amen," Uncle Roscoe said.

Uncle Roscoe talked so country, I could tell he had fake teeth in his mouth, he couldn't say his words right. Each time he talked to us his top teeth fell down on top of the bottom teeth.

{{Clink}}

Right after he finished the blessing, Uncle Roscoe slipped out the back door. Grandma Gheema didn't even see him leave. I guess he didn't want no mo surprises, LOL.

"Grandma Gheema, what's this"? Candice asked.

"Tasssssste," Grandma hissed.

"Oh no, Alex, is your pepper moving?" Candice said.

"Eww, yeah, it is."

"Sissy, how about you? Is your pepper moving?"

"No ... wait, yes, yuck! Yeah, it is."

"Calvin…?"

"You, you don't have to ask….my, my pepper is moving, moving too."

"Grandma, the pepper is moving!" I screamed.

We all jumped up from the table and pressed ourselves against the kitchen wall.

The pepper was little tiny ants, gross!

"Sit down, they will not harm you" said Grandma Gheema, raising her left eyebrow. "Eat!" she demanded.

"Whoa, Alex, your grandmother is not joking. She's crazy scary," whispered Sissy.

"I'm not eating this stuff," Candice said.

"I'm not eating it either," said Sissy with a nervous chuckle.

"Me, me either," Calvin said.

"I'll try it. How bad can it be?" I announced bravely.

I took one spoonful.

{{Slurp}}

"Jumping kangaroos, that is nasty!"

"Eww Alex, you have bug breath now, LOL." Sissy laughed.

Chapter Four

Grandma's Ghostly Hostess with the Mostess

Mom was nowhere in sight; I wondered where she could be. Grandma Gheema made us a little nervous. But maybe it was just all in our heads. Grandma left the kitchen and went into the study. It was kind of like a library–dark and drafty with lots of old books. The drapes were black and red with a gold tie-back. The furniture was all black leather, and the rug was gold. There was an old piano with candles all over it and a huge fireplace. It was as tall as the wall.

"All, all those candles, candles on the piano. Piano is a fire hazard, a fire hazard," Calvin said.

"Oh gosh! What a fashion statement in here," said Candice.

"Wow! Look, more animal heads on the wall," Sissy pointed out.

"Yeah, yeah, that is called taxi...taxidermy. They have, have the animals stuffed, stuffed for display, display," Calvin explained.

"Come in, children. Have a seat and let Grandma Gheema tell you a story."

"Grandma, how old is this house?" I asked.

"Well, Alex, it's over one hundred years old."

"Whoa!"

"When your great-grandmama and great-grandpapa first came to Woodcrack, Louisiana, they were poor and couldn't afford much. When they were looking for a place to live and build a life, they found this place in the middle of the bayou. No one wanted this old house. Your great grandparents took what little bit of money they had and made this place a home for me and my older brother, your great-uncle Thad.

"I thought Uncle Roscoe was your brother?"

"No, child, he's just someone who pops in and out from time to time.

"As I was saying, it wasn't much, but we made the best of it. At a very early age, I noticed this house had a mind of its own."

"What do you mean it had a mind of its own?" I asked concerned.

"Well, Alex dear, I would see strange things, and I would hear strange things. I would try to tell my parents, but they ignored me. My brother couldn't see the things I could. It was only me who witnessed the strange happenings in this house."

"Grandma Gheema, are you saying this house is haunted?" asked Candice.

"Well, well, if it is…. we, we need to go, go home right now," said Calvin.

"Oh Calvin, sunny boy, it's just an old house. There is nothing to be afraid of," said Grandma Gheema smiling.

"Candice, dearie, I wouldn't say it's haunted. Let's just say it's full of life."

My gal pal, Sissy, was sitting quietly with a smirk on her face. I wondered what she was thinking. Probably thought it was cool that there might be ghosts floating around here.

"What did you see that was so strange, Grandma?" I asked.

"Well, my child, I saw objects move and the water faucets turn on by themselves, and I heard footsteps in the night. This went on for a long time. But I got used to it. My parents left me this house, and this is where your mother grew up, Alex."

Mom suddenly appeared in the study room entrance, and there was one of the dolls from the hallway standing across from her. How did that get there?!?

"Yes, home sweet home," she said.

"Mom, did you like growing up here?"

"Well, Alex, it certainly was interesting. I didn't witness the things your grandmother did. I think she is the only special one. I mean she can hear and see things we can't."

"Wow! That's cool... I think!" Sissy said.

"Grandma, do you think we'll see or hear anything tonight?" I asked.

"Well, I don't know, child... Let's see," Grandma giggled.

"Nope, nope! I don't, I don't wanna see," Calvin said.

"I wanna see, I wanna see. This will be fun ... I hope," Sissy said.

"Alex, you would ask that question. I don't think I wanna see anything either," Candice said.

"Grandma, the house seems so small from the outside, but it's really big in here."

"I know child, that is one of the many mysteries of this house,"

"I'm thirsty, may I have a drink of water, Ma'am," asked Sissy.

"No need to ask, child, help yourself."

"Ahh, Alex, can you go with me?" Sissy said.

"What's the matter, Sillington? You scared?"

"No! I just thought you'd want to tag along".

"Yeah, right!"

"Whatever, Dudette."

I knew Sissy was feeling a little uneasy, so I followed her and stood right outside the kitchen without her knowing. As she grabbed a plastic cup from the cupboard, she noticed a bunch of ants.

They startled her and she dropped the plastic cup. I'm glad it wasn't glass, whew!

They were all lined up and marching along the windowsill. I didn't know where they were coming from. It looked kind of strange, but Sissy didn't think much of it.

Sissy and Calvin are somewhat alike. She likes bugs and stuff. She's such a tomboy. She's a barrel of laughs though.

"Hey Alex, can you come in here?"

I walked into the kitchen like I didn't know anything.

"Hey there, what's up, dudette?"

"Look at that!" Sissy pointed at a row of ants marching along the windowsill.

"Whoa, where are they going?"

"I don't know, but it looks weird."

"Let's get some bug spray."

"No, I don't think your grandma would want us to do that. They may be a part of the house" said Sissy. "Remember the pepper?"

"IDK, (For you dudettes out there, I don't know) you may be right, so weird." I said.

"Come on, let's get back in the study with the rest of the gang."

Sissy never did get that drink of water.

"Hey Alex, your Grandma Gheema is kind of cool, I had my doubts earlier. She had us shaking in our shoes. I was ready to go. But everything is cool now … I hope." Candice said as we walked in.

Grandma Gheema overhearing Candice laughed a wicked laugh. "That's what she thinks, you are headed for the ride of your lives, He he he he he!"

27

As Grandma looked over at the gigantic window, I noticed that the doll that had been standing in the doorway was now sitting on the windowsill.

"It moved, the doll moved again," I yelled.

Everyone just looked at me in disbelief, except for Calvin, his eyes were wide open.

Chapter Five

First Fright Night

"Okay, kiddos, it's time for you to head upstairs to bed," said Grandma Gheema.

"Aww, Grandma, do we have to? It's spring break! We don't have school tomorrow."

"Yes, Alex, I have some things for you all to do tomorrow." Grandma Gheema seemed excited.

"Mom!"

"Alex, do as your grandmother says."

"Ooo, Alex, what does she mean?" Candice said clenching her fists.

"I don't know, dudette."

"I didn't come here to do chores."

"IKR (that means I know, right). Me either."

Me, Candice, Sissy, and Calvin headed to
our rooms. Going upstairs, we passed a lot of
pictures of my ancestors. At least I think they
were my ancestors. The eyes on the pictures
looked like they were watching us as we walked
by. I tried not to look at them and neither did
my crew. We could feel that something was not
right.

We passed by five doors. One of them I guessed had to be Grandma Gheema's room. I bet it was interesting in her room. You know me, I'm nosey, so I planned to check it out later. Calvin is an antsy pants and he had to sleep in a room all by himself.

As Calvin opened the door to his room, he turned back and looked at us as if that was the last time he would see us. I felt sorry for the poor guy. He's my best bud too. We wouldn't let anything happen to him.

Me and the girls went into our room. It was old, cold, and creepy with mirrors all over the place. PERFECT for Candice, LOL! I couldn't believe how big the windows were. It was pitch-black outside. I couldn't see anything. If you looked out there for a long time, your mind and eyes would start to play tricks on you.

There were three beds and a long couch in our room. I took a bed, silly Sissy took a bed, and Princess Candice sprawled out on the bed in between me and Sissy.

The room looked dusty, but it wasn't. I looked around to see if our room had a bathroom, and it didn't. That meant we would have to go use the bathroom down the hall.

On the other side of our room, there was a big standalone closet. It was brown trimmed in gold. It looks incredibly old and expensive. What do they call stuff like that? Oh yeah, antiques. I went over to it and opened it. It was like stepping into another room, but I didn't know where it led to. I didn't say anything. I just closed the door and rejoined my gal pals.

We started talking about school.

"Candice, how about those kooky teachers we have this year?" I laughed.

"Yeah, I know, they are a trip! I mean for real, Ms. Twizzle, the Art teacher, hanging from the windowsill. I laughed so hard my sides hurt," said Candice.

"Yeah, well, I didn't find that funny. I love Ms. Twizzle. But what I did find funny was Mr. Addlow, the math teacher. I mean, who walks around with a stool the whole class?" Sissy laughed.

We talked and talked for hours, and then we all got quiet. That usually happens when us kids get sleepy and tired.

{{Snoring}}   {{Snoring}}

"Sissy! Sissy! HEY!" I called out.

Sissy had fallen asleep just that quick.

She was a brave kid. I wasn't sure I was ready to go to sleep yet.

{{BAM!}}

"You hear that?"

"Yeah, what was that?" said Candice.

I ran across the hall and burst into Calvin's room. Calvin was peeking out from under the covers chanting, "I don't believe in ghosts, I don't believe in ghosts...No, I don't believe in ghosts."

He was shaking like a leaf.

"Calvin, Calvin, are you alright?" I asked.

"Alex, I'm scared, so scared, really scared," Calvin said.

"Come on, come with me. You can sleep on the couch. It's not fair that you're all alone. You need to be with us."

We were all a little shaken and still hadn't figured out what that noise was.

While we were in Calvin's room, Sissy woke up and started yelling for us. Me, Candice, and Calvin ran back into the room, slammed the door, and locked it.

"Is everyone here," I asked.

One by one everyone responded.

Candice said, "I'm here!"

Sissy said, "I'm here!"

Calvin said, "I'm here! I'm here!"

Then another voice blurted out, "I'm here too."

"Who said that?" I yelled.

"Not, not me," said Calvin.

"Aww, peanut butter jelly!" I admit, I was scared.

"Alex, this is no time for a sandwich," Candice said.

"I know, I know, that's not what I meant......I wanna know where that extra voice came from?!?"

We were all curious and nervous. We searched the room for that extra voice, but we didn't find anyone, so we decided to go to bed.

We all jumped into our beds and Calvin settled down on the couch. We covered our faces with just our eyes peeking out. It took a while, but eventually the gang fell asleep.

But not me, I couldn't sleep. I sat up watching the crew. I wanted to investigate, but thought I'd better stay there. I was hoping to see something, so I could tell the gang.

Was I scared? Heck, yeah!

But a girl's gotta do what a girl's gotta do.

My eyes were getting heavy, but I refused to go to sleep. Something was about to happen. I could feel it, I just knew it.

UGH! Nothing was happening!

Oh well, goodnight.

Chapter Six

Attic Antics

Cock-a-doodle do, Cock-a-doodle do
Cock-a-doodle do

{{Yawn}}

I woke up before the rest of the gang. By the bathroom found some steps that led to the kitchen, and I overheard Mom and Grandma talking.

"Patricia, go wake the children," said Grandma Gheema.

"What do you have planned for them today, Mother?" asked Mom.

"Well dear, those little busy bodies are itching to see them a ghost, so I figure I'd have them clean out the attic, so they can see them a ghost." Grandma Gheema laughed.

"Ha ha! Good one, Mother!" Mom laughed, but then she considered. "They won't be too scared, will they?"

"Ha ha! No, child. Them up there are friendly ghosts."

"Oh, Mother, you still have that thick southern accent I love so dearly."

"Oh, honey child, you know I loves the south, he he!"

I ran and got back in bed before Mom reached our room. I pretended to be asleep.

Mom doesn't like when I eavesdrop. She thinks a kid should stay in their place.

Mom came into our room and abruptly yelled, "Rise and shine, sleepy heads. Grandma Gheema made some breakfast, so you can fuel up before you get started."

"Get started on what?" I rubbed my eyes.

"You guys are going to clean out the attic today."

"Huh! Are you kidding me?"

"No, ma'am, I'm not. Up and at 'em.'"

"Alex! Why do we have to clean the attic in your grandma's house. Its spring break, I wanted to go to a hair convention," Candice whined.

"Well, I guess she wants us to do some spring cleaning, lol."

"Oh, oh wow, we have to, to clean the attic. I wonder, I wonder if there are, are any ghosts up there?" Calvin said.

"Hmm, this is like that fairytale where the pretty young girl is locked away in the attic waiting for her handsome prince to rescue her, yuck!" complained Sissy.

"Hey! I'm just as unhappy as the rest of you guys. I don't want to do it, but let's make the best of it. We may find some really cool stuff up there."

"Kids! Come on! And Calvin, don't worry, Grandma Gheema said the ghosts are friendly, LOL," Mom said.

It took us a minute to get downstairs. We all needed to wash up and brush our teeth. I'm not sure why though. We were going to get dirty in the attic. Miss fresh-and-so-clean, I mean Candice, was going to itch to pieces, ha ha!

Sissy would like it though. She's into adventures.

Calvin, well, I really don't need to tell you what he was going to be like. He would be holding a flashlight waiting for a ghost to appear.

Me, Candice, Sissy, and Calvin tiptoed by the portraits on the hallway wall hoping the eyes from the pictures wouldn't follow us again, but of course, they did.

"Those darn pictures!"

"GOOD morning! I am so happy to see you're all here and no one is missing," said Grandma Gheema with a bizarre grin.

"Why, why would we be missing, be missing?" said Calvin.

"Oh, I don't know dear, but you're here and that's all that matters."

"Grandma Gheema, what did you make this time?" I asked.

"Well, Alex, I have good stuff. I have pancakes dripping with maple syrup, eggs smothered in cheese, sausage swimming in gravy, and honey baked biscuits spilling out of the pan. How does that sound, dearie?"

"Umm, Hmm, sounds yummy."

My BFFs agree, until we see that the pancakes, eggs, sausage, and biscuits are green.

Please let that be food coloring and not mold, you know like that storybook by a doctor talking about yellow eggs and ham or was it green? Anyway, something like that, yuck!

"OMG! (Oh, My Goodness) Why is it green?" Candice said.

"Oh dearie, a little mold is good for your teeth," said Grandma Gheema.

How was mold good for your teeth? Grandma's teeth were not sparkling white but had a slight greenish tint to them. Hmm…

"I hear that coal is good for your teeth, but I don't know about mold," Sissy said.

"I think I'm going to be sick. By the time we leave from here, we will all weigh a buck-o-five. I need real food," I said.

"Oh my goodness, Oh my goodness. What is happening here, happening here?" said Calvin.

I am so mad! I had my mouth all set for those pancakes dripping with maple syrup, eggs smothered in cheese, sausage swimming in gravy, and honey-baked biscuit dripping out of the pan.

"Alright, alright, sit down – Enjoy!" insisted Mom.

"Umm, hey! Not bad, not bad at all."

Every time Grandma Gheema fixed something, we thought it was going to be nasty, but it turned out to be good. Except for that bowl of soup yesterday—that was nasty! "It isn't mold, it's food coloring. Grandma Gheema got jokes!" I said relieved.

We sat there and filled our bellies with all that yummy food and to top it off we had freshly squeezed orange juice! That was the only thing that looked normal.

When we finished I got up and carried my plate to the sink. "Come on, gang, let's go see what's in the attic."

We headed up to the second floor, passing those creepy pictures again, and I thought I saw one of them wink at me. We dashed straight to the back of the old house, where we found a door— ON THE CEILING! We were told to just pull the thick rope, and it would lower a ladder.

Sissy was the first to get to the rope, and she pulled it.

"Whoa! watch out, dudette, that almost hit your head. Sissy, we don't need you to lose your head," I said.

"Yikes, I know. I need my head. I'd be lonely without it, LOL," said Sissy.

"Ha ha! Sissy, very funny."

We climbed up the ladder. It was dark and creepy. We could feel a cold draft. I felt cobwebs all over my face. The floorboards were making a creaking noise as we stepped on them one by one.

I was first in line. Candice was holding onto my shirt. Sissy was holding onto Candice's shirt, and Calvin was holding onto Sissy's shirt. I hoped nothing was holding onto Calvin's shirt. It was black as tar up here, and we searched for a light switch. I can't tell a fib, we were a little scared, so we stuck together like glue, and we couldn't move without each other. It was like we were attached at the hips.

{{SCREAMING}}

Candice screamed and startled us.

"What happened?" I yelled.

"Whew, never mind, I bumped into a mannequin. I thought it was a ghost," explained Candice.

"Ghost, ghost, oh please, no ghost up here," Calvin said.

"Sissy! Sissy!" I called.

"Huh?"

"Just checking to see if you're back there"

"Yup, I'm here, LOL. I'm not afraid of no silly ole ghost. I've never seen one. How can I be afraid of something I've never seen?" Sissy giggled.

Grandma Gheema and Mom stayed in the kitchen to wash the dishes. They were talking and playing catch up since Mom hasn't visit in a while. I could tell they were still close though. There was a certain bond they had, and Mom seemed different in her childhood home. She claimed she couldn't see what Grandma Gheema could see, but I thought she could.

I heard Grandma ask Mom why she'd stayed away so long. Mom just looked at her with teary eyes. I didn't hear her answer. I think it had something to do with my dad leaving us. Sometimes things don't always work out between our parents, and it's not our fault, it's just the way it is. Mom was sad for a long time, but she is fine now. She has me and my goofy, big brother, Andrew, and we love each other very much.

I was happy to be there visiting my Grandma Gheema, I wanted to get to know her better. Grandma Gheema seemed odd and a little scary, but she was cool. I hoped she had some more tricks up her sleeve to show us. And I bet that Grandma Gheema knew a lot.

Chapter Seven

I See That, Do You?

The attic was huge. I didn't understand how. Did you dudes and dudettes see the house on the front of this book? It's tiny! This was a straaaange place!

"Hey, where's that darn light?!?"

"I think I found it," said Candice.

"Well, turn it on!"

"Okay, okay, hold your horses."

{{CLICK}}

"Let there be light!" Sissy held her hands in the air.

"Wow, wow, look at all this, all this stuff up here," said Calvin.

"Whoa! Look at that case over there with all those dolls in it. They look like the dolls in the hallway downstairs. This one right here, she was downstairs. How did she get up here?" Candice said.

"They look a little scary, just sitting there neatly against the wall. They better not start walking or talking," I said.

"They already have. I'm telling you this one was downstairs," said Candice.

"Yikes! Do you see that?" said Calvin.

"No, what?" Sissy asked.

"One of the dolls stood up, stood up and sat back down," said Calvin.

"Okie dokie, Calvin has finally lost it," Sissy said.

"Ha ha ha, Calvin!" I said.

"Really it did, really it did," insisted Calvin.

"Stop joking around, Calvin, lets finds some other stuff to look at. Hey! Like that old brown and gold chest over there."

I pointed and the gang all ran over to open it.

{{Grunt, grunt}}

I tried to open it, but it was locked.

"Maybe that skeleton key on the wall opens it," I suggested, pointing at a large rusty key that was hanging on a hook.

"How do you know it's a skeleton key?" asked Candice.

"I don't. I just see a key and it looks kinda like a skeleton, so, why not? Ha, ha!"

"Okay, Ms. Knowitall, open it up!"

I took the key from the wall and placed it in the lock, turned it, and the chest popped open.

"Whhhhoa!"

The chest was full of jewels attached to all these funny looking clothes.

"Hey, Alex, look at me!" Sissy had taken out one of the robes and was trying it on.

"Look at all the neat colors and sparkly jewels on this thing!"

I studied the robe, then turned around and looked at the dusty attic wall covered in cobwebs. I looked at the robe again and back at the wall, and there was a fifteen-foot-tall portrait of a woman dressed like a fortune teller. The woman was fair skinned with coal black hair, had wrinkles in her face, and she wasn't smiling. Heyyy! Something like my Grandma.

Hang on, T. D. Said will help you look up fortune teller, lol.

Note: A fortune teller predicts a person's future.

"Sissy, Take that off!" I said.

"Why?" said Sissy

"Look behind you, on the wall."

"Who – is – that?"

"Hey, hey, that's, that's your great grandmother, Alex," said Calvin.

"What are you talking about, Calvin?"

"When you and Sissy were in the kitchen, were in the kitchen, your Grandma, Grandma Gheema told us a little bit about your great-grandma, Madam, Madam, Lola.

Grandma Gheema said, said she was a powerful, powerful woman, and she could make things happen. I didn't want to hear anymore; I was getting, getting nervous."

"Really, wow, interesting. I wish I had heard the story and even better, had the chance to know my Great-Grandma Lola," I said.

"Will you guys stop lollipoppin around? Aren't we supposed to be cleaning this icky place?" said Candice.

I turned and looked at the case of dolls lined up against the wall and one was missing.

"Did one of you guys move a doll from over there?" I asked.

"Alex, Alex, please stop playing," pleads Calvin.

{{SCREAMING}}

"Candice, is that you again?" I asked.

"Yesss! A mouse ran across my new white tennis shoes. Eww, I can't do this anymore," Candice said.

"Oh brother! Girls, girls, yuck!" said Calvin.

"Guys, seriously, the doll," I said.

"I don't know, who cares?" said Sissy.

"Okay, well, I'm going to put the skeleton key back on the wall."

I went to place the key back on the wall where I found it, and to my surprise a secret door opened. I jumped back and looked at my BFFs.

Sissy, Calvin, and Candice looked like they had seen a ghost. There were spiral stairs leading up to … I don't know where.

There was an organ playing.

"Where is that music coming from?" I said.

We might have been scared, but we were also curious. We grabbed each other's shirt tails and walked up the stairs one behind the other. I don't know why I am always the first in line.

As we walked up the spiral stairs, we got closer to the music. It was loud and creepy, but not as loud as the chattering from Candice's teeth.

At the top of the stairs, there was a red door that was open just a crack.

I got to it first and peeped inside, but wait! How was it that we were on another floor if we were already in the attic? It didn't make sense.

I slowly opened the door and Candice, Calvin, Sissy, and I saw an old dusty organ. And it was playing by itself.

"Oh my goodness, oh my, there's no one playing, playing that organ," said Calvin.

"Aaah! Aaah! Aaah!" we screamed together!!!

We all started to run towards the steps, but Sissy was so scared, she was running in place and not moving at all. One by one, we hopped on the banister and slid down. Me first, then Candice, then Calvin, and finally Sissy.

"Whoa!" We all screamed as we hit the floor and piled up on top of each other.

"Was that a ghost, was it, was it?" asked a panicked Calvin breathing hard.

"I don't know, but I got the heck out of there," I said.

"Okay, okay, I've had enough," said Candice. "No more cleaning in the attic."

Sliding down the rails had put us right back in the attic again. I have to admit that was a little scary and fun.

"Man, Alex, what was that all about?" said Candice.

"Idk dudette"

"Psst, psst, hey!" someone whispered.

"Do ya'll hear that?" I said.

Sissy slouched down and looked from side to side. "Did we hear what?"

"Someone said *Psst.*"

"Nooo, stop playing, Alex," Sissy said.

"I'm not. I heard someone say, *Psst.*"

"Hey! Over here, I'm on the windowsill," said the whisper.

I walked over to the windowsill, and the only thing I could see was a little black spider.

"There's no one here!"

"It was me, silly, allow me to introduce myself, I am Mr. Hobbs," said the spider.

"Wait, wait, wait, spiders don't talk,"

"Well I do, Mademoiselle, Alex".

"How do you know my name?"

"Everyone knows about little Ms. Alexandria P. Knowitall."

"Hey guys, come look at this?" I yelled.

"No need, child, you are the only one who can hear me."

"Oh great! I'm the one losing it now."

'Mademoiselle Gheema always brags about her Smart Alec Alex. That'd be you, right?" said Mr. Hobbs.

"Yes, I guess, so how is it that you can talk, and I'm the only one who can hear you?"

"Seems to me, child, you fit right in with the family. You know that thing they talk about ....?"

"No, what thing they talk about, and who is they?"

"I heard your Grandma Gheema say only certain people in this family can see and hear strange things in this attic."

"Are you saying, I am one of them?"

"That's what I'm saying, child, you're special."

"Wow! I'm not sure I want this kind of power."

"ALEX…ALEX, where are you" Sissy is yelling.

"Yeah!" I call back.

"Come on, let's get out of here."

"Oh well, I gotta go. It was nice meeting you!"

"It was my pleasure, child," said Mr. Hobbs.

Chapter Eight

Sister, Sister

"Alex, Alex, where were you, where were you, we turned around and you were gone, you were gone." said Calvin.

"I heard something, and I went to the windowsill and I... well, never mind." I tried to explain but gave up.

"What, what?" said Calvin.

"Nothing, just forget it."

I knew if I told them I was by the windowsill talking to a spider, they'd think I was kooky, so I decided I'd just keep that to myself.

The gang and I were making our way out of the attic, when...

"Whoaaa! Whee! Ouch! Hey!"

The floor opened, and we all fell through and landed in the hallway where the creepy pictures were. Their eyes were still following us.

"What in the name of beauty products happened?" said Candice.

"Wow! That was fun!" Sissy said.

"That was crazy! Why did the floor open up like that?" I said.

We got up and brushed ourselves off and started walking down the hall. I saw my mom walking towards us.

"Hi, Mom," I called out.

"Hi there, and you are?" Mom said.

"Oh, Mom, stop kidding around."

"Well, it was a pleasure meeting you. I'm sure I'll see you around."

I wondered why my mom was acting like she didn't know me.

"Wow, Alex, that was weird. What's wrong with your mom?" asked Candice.

I shrugged.

Then something odd happened. My mom was coming up the stairs again, and she was wearing different clothes.

"So, how's it going, kids? Finish in the attic?" said Mom.

"Mom?"

"Yes."

"Just a few minutes ago, you walked by and acted like you didn't know me."

"Alex, what are you talking about? I was in the kitchen with your grandmother."

"But Mom, I saw you a few minutes ago, whatever."

"Excuse me, young lady."

"Nothing, Ma'am."

"Alex, are you okay? You've been acting weird for the past hour," Candice said.

"Yeah, Alex, you have, you have. What's the matter? You're not turning into something, are you, ARE YOU?" said Calvin.

"Ha! Yeah, Calvin, I'm turning into your worst nightmare, lol."

"Kiddos come on in the kitchen. Are you hungry?" called Grandma Gheema.

Me and my BFFs walked into the kitchen and again, there is my mom. But she couldn't have beat us to the kitchen? She was upstairs going to the bathroom. But there she was sitting there calmly eating a piece of German chocolate cake. I was confused and starting to doubt myself. I scratched my head and asked myself, *am I okay*?

But all around me, everyone was acting normal. At this point, I wasn't hungry anymore.

The rest of the gang sat down and started eating. Grandma fixed something call gumbo. Everybody gets excited when you say gumbo! It's an old famous New Orleans dish. Knowing Grandma Gheema, it had everything in it *including* the kitchen sink, LOL.

But Grandma tells us what's in it: chopped veggies, sausage, garlic, shrimp, chicken's breath … Eww, what's chicken breath? Oh no, wait, Grandma said chicken *broth*, LOL. It has a lot of other weird stuff in it and the people here LOVE IT!

Me, not so much. Just give me a hamburger and fries with a chocolate milkshake and I'm happy.

Sissy, Calvin, and Candice were eating the gumbo. They liked it. They really liked it!

"Alex, Alex, you should try it, you should try it," said Calvin.

"Yum, yum, I love shrimp! You're missing out on some good stuff, dudette," insisted Sissy.

"Hey guys, I don't like to get stuff on my clothes, but I must admit, this is amazing!" added Candice.

It was like everyone was in a trance. Candice had juice from the gumbo dripping from her mouth to her shirt.

"Alex, honey, since you're not eating, you can wash the dishes," Grandma Gheema said.

"Aww, Grandma, why do I have to do the dishes? Look at this mess, my BFFs can help, right?"

"Nope! You're on your own tonight, my little pumpkin pie," said Grandma Gheema.

I looked at my mom, or at least I thought it was my mom. She seemed so strange, like she didn't know me. I was sad about that. I guess that's why I wasn't hungry.

"Mom! Do I have to do the dishes by myself?" I whined.

She wasn't answering me. She was ignoring me. She wasn't looking at me. *WHAT'S GOING ON?!?*

"Oh Alex, calm down, honey, LOL," said Mom.

My mom was standing in the kitchen doorway, so who was that woman who looked just like my mom sitting at the table?

"Hee! Hee! I guess it's time for you to meet your Aunt Priscilla, you mother's twin sister!" said Grandma.

"My two baby girls, Patricia and Priscilla,"

"Wait, What? Mom, you never told me you had a twin sister!"

I'm not the one that's kookoo. This family is kookoo.

"What a dirty trick! I thought I was losing it."

"Finally, someone got you, little Miss Knowitall," said Mom.

"Ha ha ha, very funny, Mom!"

"Hi there, Alex, I'm your Aunt Priscilla. I've heard so much about you. And what I've heard reminds me of myself when I was your age. I'm sorry we tricked you." Aunt Priscilla laughed.

"That's right, Alex, your Aunt Priscilla and you are the same. She's a Miss Smarty Pants too," said Mom.

While all this was going on, the gang was still eating. They should have been ready to burst by now. For a moment I missed those guys, and they'd missed the whole conversation. They'd never even looked up to see what was going on. I think it was planned that way. I think something was in the gumbo that made them all black out. Oh well, another day in the books at Grandma's house.

Chapter Nine

Hear No Evil, See No Evil

"Boy! What a long day. I can't believe I'm saying this, but I'm ready for bed."

Outside the wind started to pick-up, and the rain was coming down like cats and dogs. I looked out our window, and I could see the small boat we used in the bayou to get to Grandma's house was rocking back and forward from the wind. Man! What a spooky scene.

Everyone was in their rooms for the night when I heard the doorbell. I peeked my head out in the hallway to see if Mom, Grandma, or Aunt Priscilla was going to answer the door, but they were nowhere in sight. The gang was talking and playing some hip-hop music and dancing.

Ha-ha! {Laughter in the background}Ha-ha!

"Shhh, you guys hear that?" I said.

"Come on, Alex, dance with us. Stop being a saggy drag," said Sissy.

"No, wait… listen!"

{{Ding Dong ~ Ding Dong Ding}}

"Someone's at the door, and it's almost midnight. Who in jumping jack flash would be out in the middle of this creepy dark place?"

"Ooh, maybe this is our chance to see a ghost," Sissy said.

"Nope, nope, nope! If so, I'll pass, I'll pass," said Calvin.

"Well, come on, let's see who it is," said an excited Sissy.

"I'll stay, stay up here," Calvin said.

"No, dude, we all go together," I said.

We tiptoed down the hall, and one by one we rode the banister down the stairs.

{{Ding Dong ~ Ding Dong Ding}}

I moved closer to the door and took a chair with me to stand on, so I could peek through the peephole. I was scared to look, so I closed my eyes, then opened them slowly, in case I was startled, but I didn't see anything.

My BFFs were standing behind me. They were as scared as I was. I stepped down off the chair and opened the door slowly.

"HELLO! ANYBODY THERE? HELLO!" I called out.

This time, Me, Candice, Sissy, and Calvin peeked out the front door together, and we still couldn't see anything, except for millions of fireflies over the swamp near Grandma's house.

"Al, Al, Alex, who's that, who's that over there?" Calvin pointed.

We turned to see what Calvin was talking about, and we all saw a woman in black walking through the woods towards the back of Grandma's house. It almost looked like she was floating in the night air.

We stepped out of the house and scaled the walls of the front porch, like the great moose detective, to follow the woman, but she disappeared before we could catch up to her.

We ran back in the house so fast, locked the front door, and ran all the way to our room and locked that door too. I looked at Candice who was pointing at the window.

"Ah, ah, Alex, I think I see our ghost"

I walked over to where Candice was standing and looked out the window and there she was, the woman in black.

We all screamed and jumped into our beds and pulled the covers over our heads.

{{KNOCK, KNOCK, KNOCK}}

"What's going on in here?" said Grandma Gheema.

"Grandma, Grandma, look out the window. You see her, the woman in black. Is she a ghost?"

"Oh child, is that who you're screaming about? Why, that's just little old Mrs. Maynon. She walks the grounds at night for exercise. She sometimes rings my doorbell to let me know she's out there, he-he-he!"

"That's weird, the gators don't bother her?"

"I guess not, he-he-he! See you kiddies in the morning."

Calvin was so spooked, he couldn't sleep. He sat straight up on the couch where we were allowing him to sleep.

"Calvin, try to sleep. We're going to the gator farm tomorrow," I said.

"Oh, brother, oh brother!" said Calvin.

Chapter Ten

The Gator Farm

Despite having the bees cheese scared out of us, LOL, we were having the time of our lives. Grandma Gheema was loads of fun and her stories were amazing. Her food was funny looking, but it was good. My BFFs thought she was so cool. And it had been a while since my mom had been happy in her surroundings. I know sometimes she thought about the good times with my dad. But things were looking up, and she'd been doing fine.

My mom is the best! I hope she and Aunt Priscilla keep in touch from now on. Aunt Priscilla is great too.

"Alex hon! How's school, and what activities are you planning to participate in?" Aunt Priscilla asked.

"Oh, hey, Aunt Priscilla! Well, it's spring break at T.K. Spittle Middle School. IDK, I haven't given it much thought."

"Well, you know, honey, it's good to be in those activities. You probably think I don't know much because I'm down here in these sticks, but I know a thing or two," Aunt Priscilla said.

"Why? It's a not big deal, right?"

"Yes, indeed it's a big deal. It's great to be involved, it prepares you for lots of things, but for now, have fun!"

"Well, I was going to try out for the cheerleading team, just to prove a point."

"And what is it that you need to prove, child?"

"Well, folks think that because I'm in sixth grade I can't hang with the big girls, so why not try out and prove them wrong?"

"Okay, then, go for it! But honestly, I would think your friend Candice would be more the cheerleader type."

"Yeah, all the better for me to do it. It's expected of Candice, but not me."

"Alright, I get it. Best of luck to ya!"

"Thanks, Auntie, how do you know so much?"

"Welllll... I didn't tell you, but I'm a teacher at the University here."

"Wow! that's great. Maybe I can go to your university when I grow up?"

"Maybe, but remember......you gotta be involved in activities, so you can become well-rounded."

"Got it, Auntie!"

"Well, you guys have a great day! I have some papers to grade."

"Whoa, were you dudes and dudettes listening to my conversation with my Aunt Priscilla? I hope you are doing a lot in school to be well rounded, ha-ha! Yeah, I'm talking to you, reader."

"Come on here, kiddies and grab a pair of galoshes (that's boots, dudes and dudettes)," said Grandma Gheema.

"I, I wonder why we need, we need boots, need boots?" said Calvin.

Grandma and Mom were taking us to a gator farm. If you've seen one gator you've seen them all. I wanted to do something different, something fun! The gator farm was dirty and wet, that's why Grandma told us to grab our galoshes. I'm a city kid. I wanted to go to an amusement park and eat hot dogs and candy, play games and win big fluffy stuffed animals. I didn't think they'd have anything like that in the gator park.

"All aboard," said Mom.

"Aww man! Are you kidding? We have to get in that grim-reaping boat again?"

Me and the gang hopped into the boat. It was rocking back and forth like crazy. It felt like we were going to tip over. This time Candice didn't complain about her hair and nails, Calvin seemed a little more relaxed, and Sissy was just Sissy, silly and always laughing.

Grandma and Mom rowed the boat since they were bigger and faster. In no time we were on the land of the living. On the side of the river where Grandma lives, there were just a few old run-down houses. I know the woman in black lives in one of them.

"Here, here you go ladies, ladies," said Calvin.

"When did you become a polite gentleman, Calvin Clueless?" said Candice.

"I am a gentleman," protested Calvin.

"Wait! Did Calvin just complete a sentence without repeating it?" Sissy laughed.

"Ha ha ha...... I do believe you're right!" I said.

"Alright, alright, alright, pipe down, guys. Get in the car. It's only a fifteen-minute drive," said Mom.

I was sleepy, so I took a small nap on the ride over to the gator farm.

We pulled into the parking lot, and there were people all around wearing gator hats. They looked kind of cool. The big sign said, "WELCOME TO FORREST GAVIN GATOR FARM."

Mom went to the front gate to get our tickets, and the guy at the entrance put color coded bands on our wrists. The blue ones allowed you to do the boat ride and lunch. The red ones allowed you to do the boat ride, lunch, feed the gators, and watch a show. Mom bought us the red bands.

"Hey, let's feed the gators first," said Sissy.

"Eww, do you see what they are feeding them? It's raw meat, yuck!" Candice pouted.

"GIRLS! Oh brother, oh brother!" Calvin shook his head.

"Really, Calvin? You're scared of your own shadow," Candice said.

"Whatever, whatever, dudette!" Calvin said.

This park was so small we were able to ride the boat in the swamp full of gators, eat bologna sandwiches for lunch, feed the gators raw meat, and watch this man almost get his arms bitten off playing around with a large gator all within an hour and a half. I hoped Mom hadn't spent too much on this, ha ha ha!

"Hey, we didn't get our gator hats!" I yelled.

Grandma Gheema had been quiet during the trip. I guess she'd just wanted to get out of the house with us today.

"Four Gator hats coming right up!" she said.

"THANK YOU, GRANDMA!" we yelled.

Chapter Eleven

The Spirits We Met

We finally made it back to Grandma's house. But wait, we didn't use that grim-reaping boat this time. Had they pulled the wool over our eyes, again? (Meaning, had they tricked us?).

"Okay, kiddies, out you get," Mom said.

"Grandma, do you have some snacks for us?" I was hungry after our trip.

"Yes, child. But you'd better be good. You don't want Grandma putting a spell on you. He he! Double bubble, stay out of trouble!" Grandma Gheema wiggled her fingers and cackled.

We walked into the house and made a B-line (that means straight) into the kitchen to look for snacks. When I passed by the big mirror in the

foyer, I thought I saw a reflection of kid walking in the opposite direction from me. I wondered what that was about. But I wasn't ever going to ask.

"Oh yeah, oh yeah, oh yeah!" sang Sissy. "Look at all the different chips: honey barbeque, sour cream, salt and vinegar. I love them all."

"Oh no, not my chocolate cream cakes! Chocolate makes me break out in pimples, but I love my chocolate cream cakes." Candice pouted.

"Where is, where is the beef jerky?" Calvin peered at the snacks.

"Why do you want beef jerky, Calvin?" I asked.

"It's a man thing! It's a man thing! You wouldn't understand," said Calvin.

"Oh yeah, well you're far from that, buddy boy. Here you go, have a banana marshmallow pie, ha-ha!"

The gang and I started upstairs to our room. There was nothing else to do, and we were bored.

We chomped on our snacks and played some music. Candice and I started to talk about some of the cute boys in school. Who she liked and who I liked. Sissy is not at that point yet. Calvin is bashful, but I know there is one girl he really likes. She likes all the same things he likes, and she's smart as a whip.

{{Clink, Clink, Clink}}

"Shhh, quiet!"

"Hey, why did you turn the music down?" asked Sissy.

{{Clink, Clink, Clink}}

"That's why.".

"Hey dudette, what's that?" Sissy asked.

"IDK, but it sounds like it's coming from the basement, I think. It sounds like someone is banging on the pipes," Candice said.

The clinking sound was faint, but we could hear it echoing throughout the house.

"Well, well, it can just stay, stay in the basement," said Calvin.

"Come on, gang, let's go investigate.

Everyone put on your tie-dye shirts. Ghosts don't like bright colors, and tie-dye shirts have tons of colors on them," I explained.

"How do you know ghost don't like tie dye, Miss Know-it-all?" said Candice.

"Um … I don't really, but we're scared, and we have to believe in something, LOL."

I opened the bedroom door, and we headed out to find the basement.

Again, we all slid down the banister. That was so much fun!

We passed by a telephone, and Candice picked it up and yelled "Hello operator, Help! This is the vacation from... hello operator, help!"

Grandma Gheema's house is oddly shaped. The basement is right off the kitchen. I'd thought Grandma and Mom were in the kitchen talking, but they weren't. I found the door to the basement, and we all just stood looking at it as if it is going to open itself.

{{Clink, Clink, Clink}}

The clinking noise was getting louder
Yes, yes, yes, I was scared!

{{Screech}}

I opened the basement door. It was dark, cold, and smelled awful.

"Calvin, you go first. You're the man of the group."

"Uh, uh, earlier, earlier you said I wasn't, wasn't there yet."

"What do you mean, dude?"

"I'm not, I'm not a man, a man yet."

"I'll go," volunteered Sissy.

My girl!

Everyone hung on to each other's tie-dye shirts.

"Are we sure it's safe?" asked Candice.

"If it's not, we'll find out soon enough." I replied.

{{Clink, Clink, Clink}}

"What is that?"

We tiptoed down the stairs. And just like in the attic, there was a bunch of old junk all over the place. In the far-right corner, a window was open, and a branch was hitting the rusted pipes.

"Phew! So that's where the sound is coming from."

"Ah, guys…guys… GUYS!" said Candice,

"What?"

"Please tell me I'm not the only one who sees floating candles?"

She was right. There were a bunch of candles just floating in the air.

We all started to run away from them and bumped into each other and WHAM! We hit the floor.

{{Chirp, Chirp, Chirp, Chirp}}

"Boy, I hear birds chirping around my head," said Sissy.

I heard someone talking......

"Yes, yes."

"I know, I know."

"They are my best friends, my best friends."

"No, I don't, I don't think so."

"It's just something I do."

"Calvin, who are you talking to?"

"Huh? oh it's … it's my new friend, Jeremy, Jeremy."

"Ugh! What new friend? We're the only ones down here."

"Him, see, him".

{{SCREAM!!}}

"That's no friend, that's a ghost, lunkhead!"

"Hi, don't be afraid. I won't hurt you. My name is Jeremy, and you're Alex. I've wanted to meet you for a while."

"How do you know my name?"

"Your Grandma Gheema talks about you all the time."

Ugh, I've got to talk to Grandma. Seems all her permanent visitors know me.

"What are you doing down here, Jeremy?"

"What, wait, what? Jeremy is a ghost, Jeremy is a Ghoooooosst!" Calvin hit the floor as he passed out in shock.

"Thirty years ago, I was down here looking for my toy and got trapped and no one found me," said Jeremy.

"Did you live here?"

"No, I was playing with my ball and it rolled down the cellar steps. When the cellar door closed, it locked. I yelled for help, but no one could hear me. I've been stuck down here for a long time."

"So how do you know my Grandma Gheema?"

"She was always nice to me and I liked talking to her."

"Yeah, my Grandma is pretty interesting."

"Alex, Calvin, where are you guys?" said Candice.

"Well, I better go now. Your friends are calling you."

"But… wait …"

"Bye." Jeremy faded out.

"Ooo, my head, my head, what happened?" Calvin sat up slowly rubbing his head.

"Nothing, let's go," I said.

We were still a little spooked when we heard a rocking sound.

{{Creek, rock…Creek, rock…Creek, rock…Creek, rock}}

We followed the sound and found a chair rocking all by itself. We froze and watched as slowly a man appeared in the chair out of nowhere.

"What do we do now, guys? Do we scream? Do we run? Do we do anything?" Sissy said with a nervous giggle.

"Ha ha ha! No need to run. I'm Mr. Joe. Mr. Joe loves visitors, it's lonely down here sometimes. Hey there, Alex."

"Let me guess, Grandma Gheema, right?"

"Ha ha ha, yep! We go way back, your Grandma and me."

"So, what happened to you?"

"Well, I use to care for the grounds here. I was cleaning up down here when the old ticker gave out on me one day. I was so dang mad. I thought I had plenty of time left, but the big guy in the sky had other plans."

"Really…really, so we're talking to ghosts now?" said Candice.

"Yup, yup, that's what it looks like, looks like. At least they're friendly," Calvin said.

"Okay now, you kids stay out of trouble, you hear. I'll be seeing you around."

"This is amazing. I'm having the time of my life, yeah!" Sissy sings.

Chapter Twelve
Almost Over

"Shh! You're too loud," said a calm voice from the other side of the basement.

"Who's there," I whispered.

"I'm Jasper, the scaredy-cat ghost."

"Why are we whispering, Jasper, the scaredy-cat ghost?" I giggled.

"I don't like a lot of noise, so keep your voice down, Alex, please."

"Let me guess, Grandma Gheema talks about me?"

"No, I heard Mr. Joe call out you name."

"Okay, Jasper, what's your story?"

"I don't have a story. This house just looks like a friendly creepy place. I walk the earth in search of good deeds, so I can collect my wings and be free."

"You have to have a story. You're a ghost, right?"

"Yes, I am."

"So, what happened to you?"

Candice whispered in my ear. She thought Jasper was cute. You see, Jasper looks our age: 11-12 years old. I giggle. Fat change in her being his girlfriend!

"I developed an illness at a very young age, and it made me really sick. I went into the hospital, and that's all I remember. When I woke up, my mom and dad were crying."

"Bummer, I'm sorry to hear that, Jasper. You would have fit right in with the crew here."

"Thanks, Alex, that means a lot. Grandma Gheema is alone most times. She's a sweet old lady. I'll stick around here in case she needs my help. Hope to see you guys around again someday."

"Well, Jasper, it's getting late, and we've got to get back upstairs before my mom and grandma come looking for us. You take care!"

We found our way back to the stairs in the dark. We found Grandma and Mom at the kitchen table talking.

"Well, well, well, hello there, kids, spending time in the basement? Meet any interesting people? Any ghosts down there?" Grandma Gheema chuckled.

I looked at Grandma suspiciously. You know Grandma got jokes.

"As a matter of fact, we did, LOL," I say laughing.

"Really Alex?" said Mom.

"Yeah, Mom, we really did. There was Mr. Joe and…"

"Enough, Honey. You guys need to go upstairs and pack. We are heading back home tomorrow. You have school Monday."

"Okay, Mom. I'm starving! What's for dinner?"

"I ordered pizza. Is that okay?"

"Yay!" we all scream.

"I hope the delivery guy doesn't drop it in the swamp. LOL," I said.

"Come on, gang, let's go and start packing."

"You don't have to ask me twice. I can't wait to get my hair done when I get home," said Candice.

"Oh yeah, I can smell the heat on your hair already," I said.

"Oh goodie, goodie, I'll have two days to spend at the city sports and learning center," said Sissy.

"And I, and I will get to add to my bug collection, bug collection. I can finally look, look for the Papua Golden Scarab Beetle, Beetle," said Calvin.

"Yeah, I'm ready to get back home too. It's been fun, but I gotta run," I said.

That night, me and my BFFs chat about the rest of the school year. I remembered what my Aunt Priscilla had said about being well-rounded. The gang hadn't been listening to my talk with my aunt, so I had to school them (that mean teach them) on how important it is that we get involved in school.

Me, I'm just going to try-out for everything.

I gotta be me, yeah!

I plan on coming back and spending more time with my grandma. She's so cool. I want to get to know my Aunt Priscilla too. I'm sure I can learn a thing or two from her.

After saying goodbye to them, we were back on the road again. Mom seemed happier. I hope she stays close in touch with her family. Family is very important. Sometimes, they are all we have. We may not always get along but, if we don't have our family, who do we have? It was a long ride back. But me and my BFFs had so much to laugh and talk about.

As a surprise for us all, Mom decided to stop at The Great Loose Goose Lodge, a big water park, for a few hours.

We had the time of our lives splashing around in the huge wave pool. We were even brave enough to slide down some of the biggest water slides. Boy! This spring break was a hoot and a holler. I couldn't wait for next year.

"Wake-up everybody, we're home!" said Mom.

"Thanks Mrs. K, Mrs. K. Our trip was fun, was fun!" Calvin said.

"Yeah! I had a good time, Mrs. K.," said Candice.

"This trip was awesome-sauce, Mrs. K. You really know how to have fun!" Sissy said.

"Yeah Mom, this sure was interesting. Thanks for taking me to meet my family!" I said.

"Well, I am glad you all had a wonderful time. And Alex, I thought it was time for you to learn about our family. Now back to the grind!" Mom said.

There was a moving van parked across the street when we arrived home.

"Hmm, looks like we have a new neighbor," Mom said.

"Yeah, and they are right next to you, Candice girl!"

"Oh great, I hope they are good neighbors."

"Look, look, look, there is a boy our age," I said.

"Yeah, not bad," said Candice.

"Oh well, see you at school tomorrow," I said.

The next day, me and Candice ride the bus to school as normal. And as usual, Principle Hardhead is front and center with all his "Hellos" to the students as we arrive.

"Hey Candice, isn't that the new kid from our block?"

"Yeah, it is. I guess he'll be going to T.K. Spittle Middle School with us."

"Hey Alex, Hey Candice. We have a new student. Meet my cousin Aaron. I'm kind of showing him around." says Sissy.

"Ha ha! But my friends call me Arrogant Aaron, ha ha!"

"LOL, looks like you have a little competition, Ms. Knowitall, LOL," says Candice.

Oh, Brother! This is going to be very interesting.

The End!

Author Bio

Taunya T.D. Said writes children chapter books for ages 8-12.

She will keep you bent over in laughter in her Smart Alec Alex Series. Taunya has released two books in her series: *Smart Alec Alex, Changing Schools and Classroom Rules* and *Smart Alec Alex, Braces and Glassed, Imagine That!* Still a kid at heart, Taunya will be releasing more books in this hilarious series. Taunya resides in Northern Maryland with her loved ones.

Available Titles

Changing Schools and Classroom Rules

Braces AND Glasses, Imagine That!

The Vacation From...
Hello Operator, HELP!

Upcoming Titles

Cheerleading Into Some Mess.

The Acting Bug That Bit Me, Youch!

Don't Stress, It's Just A Test

The Vacation from...
Hello – Operator, Help!

P	I	T	B	A	S	E	M	E	N	T	I	F	Q	Z	S	X
A	S	P	R	I	N	G	B	R	E	A	K	L	G	B	R	D
T	R	X	U	N	C	L	E	R	O	S	C	O	E	W	V	M
R	O	P	T	W	I	N	S	N	Q	T	E	A	S	G	N	M
I	C	E	B	R	H	C	H	E	S	T	Q	T	P	H	K	G
C	K	P	G	H	O	S	T	C	R	J	T	I	O	O	T	R
I	I	P	A	W	I	O	D	L	K	E	M	N	O	S	T	A
A	N	E	P	Q	Q	C	G	U	U	R	I	G	K	T	A	N
G	G	R	Q	R	S	N	P	S	X	E	R	C	Y	D	D	D
A	C	A	A	T	T	I	C	S	M	M	R	A	S	O	V	M
T	H	N	S	Z	P	R	R	L	R	Y	O	N	O	G	E	A
O	A	T	V	O	G	E	D	U	J	S	R	D	U	M	N	G
R	I	S	C	A	R	E	D	R	O	A	S	L	N	N	T	H
F	R	G	L	R	V	G	P	W	E	F	S	E	D	Z	U	E
A	T	W	S	P	I	D	E	R	S	T	Y	S	S	O	R	E
R	O	A	D	T	R	I	P	I	E	O	B	O	A	T	E	M
M	P	R	I	S	C	I	L	L	A	P	J	U	L	I	S	A

adventures	ghost dog	roadtrip
Attic	Grandma Gheema	rocking chair
basement	Jeremy	scared
boat	mirrors	spiders
chest	Mr. Joe	spooky sounds
Floating candles	Patricia	pring break
gator farm	pepper ants	Twins
Ghost	Priscilla	Uncle Roscoe

Word Scramble

1. LEAX　＿＿＿＿＿＿＿＿＿＿＿＿
2. AVTCIAON　＿＿＿＿＿＿＿＿＿＿＿＿
3. SYSSI　＿＿＿＿＿＿＿＿＿＿＿＿
4. NACVLI　＿＿＿＿＿＿＿＿＿＿＿＿
5. NCAEDIC　＿＿＿＿＿＿＿＿＿＿＿＿
6. DRAGNMA AHEEGM　＿＿＿＿＿＿＿＿＿＿＿＿
7. GSOHT　＿＿＿＿＿＿＿＿＿＿＿＿
8. ITATC　＿＿＿＿＿＿＿＿＿＿＿＿
9. RATGO MAFR　＿＿＿＿＿＿＿＿＿＿＿＿
10. NSTA　＿＿＿＿＿＿＿＿＿＿＿＿
11. TSSIER SSTRIE　＿＿＿＿＿＿＿＿＿＿＿＿
12. SUHEO　＿＿＿＿＿＿＿＿＿＿＿＿
13. AMFLYI　＿＿＿＿＿＿＿＿＿＿＿＿
14. RCLIILSAP　＿＿＿＿＿＿＿＿＿＿＿＿
15. AIPIACTR　＿＿＿＿＿＿＿＿＿＿＿＿

Sister Sister	Vacation	Family
Gator Farm	Attic	Sissy
House	Patricia	Alex
Calvin	Ghost	Grandma Gheema
Ants	Priscilla	Candice

Color Me!

Alex

Color Smart Alec Alex's Team
Calvin, Candice, Alex and Sissy

Made in the USA
Columbia, SC
23 August 2024

41044822R00064